For Granny and Katy
–DDM

For Tasha
–AV

ZONDERKIDZ

The Story of the Easter Robin
Copyright © 2010 by Dandi Daley Mackall
Illustrations © 2010 by Anna Vojtech

Requests for information should be addressed to:

Zonderkidz, *Grand Rapids, Michigan 49530*

Library of Congress Cataloging-in-Publication Data

Mackall, Dandi Daley.
   The Story of the Easter Robin / by Dandi Daley Mackall; [illustrated
by Anna Vojtech].
      p. cm. --
   Summary: Tressa is worried that the robins nesting on her grandmother's window ledge will not survive a pre-Easter cold snap, but
her grandmother urges her to trust that God is caring for them, as
a robin once cared for His son, Jesus.
   ISBN 978-0-310-71331-9 (jacketed hardcover)
   [1. Robins--Fiction. 2. Grandmothers--Fiction. 3. Faith--Fiction.
4. Jesus Christ--Fiction. 5. Easter--Fiction.]   I. Title.
PZ7.M1905Leh 2010
                                                2006020988

Editor: Barbara Herndon
Art direction and design: Kris Nelson

Printed in China

10 11 12 13 / LPC / 5 4 3 2 1

The Story of the EASTER ROBIN

WRITTEN BY

Dandi Daley Mackall

ILLUSTRATED BY

Anna Vojtech

ZONDERkidz

ZONDERVAN.com/
AUTHORTRACKER
follow your favorite authors

What's the matter with her, Gran?" Tressa and her grandmother had watched two robins carry twigs, cat hair, and string to build a nest on Gran's window ledge. Now the bird wiggled, tail twitching while its red-orange breast rose and fell.

"That mama's just molding her nest for a good fit," Gran answered.

But Tressa worried. It was still two weeks until Easter. A million things could go wrong when a robin tried to nest this early.

The next day Tressa ran straight to Gran's after school. Gran showed her the surprise. In the center of the nest lay one perfect egg, the color of a spring sky. The father robin sat on a branch nearby, guarding his family. Tressa spotted raccoon tracks below and a blue jay eyeing the nest. "Gran, how are we going to keep the egg safe?"

"We'll have to leave that one to the Creator," Gran said.

Over the next three days, the robin laid three more eggs. Tressa watched the mother robin nudge her eggs before huddling onto them again.

"Turning her eggs keeps them from freezing," Gran explained. "See that bare spot on her red breast? God made her so she could warm her babies through that brood patch."

Tressa hoped that would be enough.

The day before Easter a cold snap hit. Frost laced the windowpane and whitened the nest. "Now the eggs will never hatch, Gran!" Tressa cried.

"We'll have to trust the one who watches the sparrow and robins," Gran said. "Now come with me. It's about time we saw to some other eggs."

Gran got some eggs from her refrigerator. She poked tiny holes in the top and bottom of each egg. Then she blew the gooey insides into a bowl, leaving the shells in one piece. "I'll show you how to make *oschter-foggel*, Easter birds. It's an old Pennsylvania Dutch tradition I learned from *my* granny."

Tressa blew half-heartedly on her egg. All she could think about were the real eggs outside in the cold.

Gran dipped her egg into blue-tinted water. When she lifted the shell from the dye, it was robin's egg blue.

Tressa knew Gran—and God—cared as much about those baby robins as she did. And Gran wasn't worried. Tressa tried blowing out her egg again. This time it worked.

Gran grinned over at her. "Since we have robins on our minds, how would you like to hear the legend behind the robin's red breast?"

Tressa dipped her egg into the dye while Gran began her story…

Around two thousand years ago, a plain
brown robin was flying over Jerusalem when
he heard angry shouts from the streets below.
Swooping down to *see* what the fuss was about,
he caught sight of a man, beaten and bent
under the weight of a wooden cross.

I know this man, thought the robin. All *earth's*
creatures, except humans, recognized Jesus—
the Creator-God come to earth.

At first the robin thought he saw a nest on Jesus' head. But when he soared closer, he understood. The "nest" was a cruel crown of thorns. *I must help the Master!* thought the robin. But what could he do?

Jesus stumbled as a whip snapped. He fell, and the thorny crown dug into his head. The robin, filled with compassion, flew at the crown and tried to knock it off Jesus' head. But the crown wouldn't budge.

It was then that the robin noticed one long thorn sticking into Jesus' forehead. The bird gathered its strength, grabbed the thorn in its beak, and tugged.

The thorn gave way. And as it came out, a drop of Jesus' blood fell onto the robin's breast, staining it red from that day to this.

$\mathcal{E}$ver since," Gran said, "the robin's red breast reminds us of Christ's sacrifice and how much he cares. The robin's song is the first sign of spring, helping us remember that after Christ died, he rose again on that first Easter."

Tressa insisted they color the rest of the eggs robin's egg blue. Gran taught her how to cut wings, heads, and tails for the Easter birds they'd hang from trees in the morning.

When Tressa woke up on Easter morning, she ran to Gran's to hang their Easter birds. As she tiptoed beneath the robins' nest, something crunched under her shoe. Jagged chips of blue shell lay scattered over the ground.

"Gran!" she cried as she burst into the house. "The eggs! They're broken!"

$\mathcal{G}$ran called Tressa up to her room. "Take a look."

Under the mother robin's wing sat four scrawny baby robins, eyes closed and mouths wide open. "They're alive!" Tressa exclaimed. She watched the daddy robin drop bits of food into the babies' mouths.

"God takes care of his creatures," Gran whispered.

*T*hrough the windowpane, Tressa could see the robins' red breasts, bright against the sunrise. She was sorry she'd ever doubted God's care. From then on, whenever she saw a robin or felt worried, she'd think of the legend. And she'd remember all Jesus went through on that first Easter.

"Thank you," she prayed, "for the robins… and for Jesus."

Outside the wind howled, but the robins' joyful chirping came through loud and true. To Tressa, it sounded like they were wishing her a happy Easter.

She answered them. "Happy Easter to you too!"

About the story of the
EASTER ROBIN

*The legend of the robin's red breast is an old Pennsylvania Dutch tale.
The point of the legend is a celebration of the robin's compassion and of Christ's sacrifice.*

*The Pennsylvania Dutch are also given credit for bringing egg coloring to the
United States, and for being the first to decorate trees with Easter birds.
We can use traditions and symbols to strengthen our faith and help us remember.*

*The robin is a sign of spring, and it can remind us of
Christ's love for us, his death, and resurrection.*

*Birds' nests help us remember Christ's crown of thorns.
The first Easter baskets were made to look like nests.*

The robin's red breast is a symbol of Christ's suffering and love.

Easter eggs remind us of our new life in Christ.